EVERYTHING THAT HAS BEEN SHALL BE AGAIN

EVERYTHING THAT HAS BEEN SHALL BE AGAIN

THE REINCARNATION FABLES OF JOHN GILGUN

WITH NINE WOOD ENGRAVINGS BY MICHAEL MCCURDY

THE BIELER PRESS 1981 *ST PAUL*

Some of the fables in this collection were previously published in
the following periodicals: *Wormwood Review* ('Mouse'),
Paragraph ('Peacock'), *Four Quarters* ('Fox'),
Phoebe ('Bear'), *Pequod* ('Gnat'),
& *Floating Island* ('Ant').

Designed by Gerald Lange.

This project has been supported, in part, through a grant
from the National Endowment for the Arts
in Washington, D C, a federal agency.

LIBRARY OF CONGRESS CATALOGING IN PUBLICATION DATA

Gilgun, John.
Everything that has been shall be again.

1. Animals, Legends and stories of.
I. McCurdy, Michael.   II. Title.
PS3557.I353E93   813'.54   81-10194   AACR2

ISBN 0-931460-13-1 (pbk.)   ISBN 0-931460-11-5 (lim. ed.)

Dedicated to Larry B. Williams

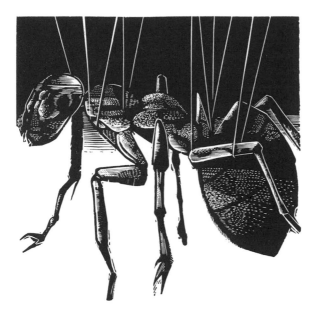

ANT

MY NAME IS AKAH-KI. I am an ant, a worker, one of the
Sterile Sisterhood. Names are forbidden to workers by
the Party. We are given numbers instead. I refuse to acknowledge my number and insist on my name. This is
my crime, for which I am being punished. I refuse to acknowledge it as a crime. My refusal to acknowledge it
as a crime is, of course, another crime. I am not really
speaking to you. I am carrying on a monologue within
my own head. I can no longer see or feel the walls of
my cell. My interrogators have snipped away the ap-

pendages I utilized formerly to perceive the world around me—funiculus, scape, frontal lobes, compound eyes. They have even excavated and sterilized my antennal fossa. But they could not get at my inner voice. That voice is all I have now. When it stops, I will cease to exist. I am suspended from the ceiling of my cell in a basket woven of silken threads generated in the bodies of my interrogators. I can still rub my tarsal claws over the threads. I imagine this makes a rasping noise distracting to my interrogators, who sit below me waiting for me to repent. But I will never repent. In this state of total sensory deprivation, I have never felt more alive, for my visions come more and more frequently now, and for the first time in my life I am more fertile than my Queen. Of course I am giving birth not to eggs but to ideas. This is a crime. I will never acknowledge it as a crime. I am a very special ant, a poet, a prophet, a revolutionary, the first to appear among the *Mesoponera castanea* in the last three million years. I have indicated to my fellows the next step in our evolutionary development. This is a crime. But change is inevitable, even among ants, and I have foreseen that change.

I remember the morning I woke in Tunnel X27 and realized that I had been metamorphosed into an ant. The transition from whatever creature I had been before to "ant" had been very rapid. I was thrown forward on legs unable to bear my weight and searing pains shot through my tibiae. I was looking down into a tunnel and my feet were planted firmly on the floor but, because of my angle of vision, I felt that I was falling. Fear was the only emotion I was capable of at that moment. An intoxicating nest odor drifted up from the depths of the tunnel. Instinctively I moved toward it. But I was stopped before I had gone very far by a member of the Sterile Sisterhood. She felt me all over, decided I was one of them and led me along Odor Trail 246-B to the Center of the Nest. I am surprised at my capacity to recall that number, but the ability to recollect Odor Trail numbers is the last thing an ant forfeits before he dies. At the Center, I was put to work instantly, feeding the Queen—an enormous black bladder, huffing, puffing and germinating in the middle of the overheated chamber. I felt an immediate, deep-seated revulsion when confronted with my Queen and this, I knew even then, went against one of the basic characteristics of ant nature. The other workers sang hymns of praise to her as they labored. I could have sung with them, but I decided to remain silent. So my differences were evident from the start. I'm sure that somewhere on the edge of the milling swarm a member of the secret police had already made note of my number—which had begun to emerge on my postpetiole—and that an alarm signal was being transferred to others further up the line. But it would be a while before they picked me up. They wanted to give me plenty of rope with which I could suspend myself from this ceiling. Ha!

From the very first day I loved my sisters for their distinguishing characteristics—the mole on the clypeus, the scar on the pronotum, the distinctive malocclusion between two mandibles which set off '3459' from '842.' I could not love the generic qualities which simply denote "ant." Need I point out that this is a crime. During our first lunch break together, I amused my sisters by juggling trophic eggs, cracking jokes and dancing. I showed them how to laugh. After lunch they did not feed the Queen with quite the same enthusiasm. I am sure the Queen didn't notice, being too busy breeding. But members of the secret police miss nothing. The slightest deviation from the routine sets them off. The following day I noticed that several sisters were missing from our line. I knew I was to blame, but something drove me forward. I had a mission. I was possessed by my vision. I could not conform. On the third day I found myself ripping political posters off the walls and chewing them into pulp. It had gone that far, yes, and, oh, so very quickly!

Yes, I loved my sisters, loved them and pitied them, the poor bedraggled drudges! They did the work which kept the hill humming and as a result they were looked down upon by those indolent—and *insolent!*—winged, thin-waisted males. I remember my rage when I first saw groups of males gathered at the intersections of tunnels, strutting about, preening themselves, exhibiting their thoraxes and sneering at my sisters for their "inadequacies." (Workers have puny, undeveloped thoraxes.)

And my sisters were even denied the pleasures of sex. We had been programmed for work, not play. The folk saying was, "A male may strut and have his fun but a sister is sterile 'cause there's work to be done."

At the end of the first week I called a cell meeting. Seventeen sisters showed up and I spoke to them on the subject "The Coming Revolution in the Hill." I was not concerned with simply setting up another nest somewhere else (under certain circumstances the bureaucracy permits this), but in destroying the hill entirely. I told my sisters, "We will emerge into the open air as a separate species, transformed physically and spiritually, worker ants no longer, but gods, gods in our own right!"

But I could not hold my audience. I ended by juggling trophic eggs again and afterwards we all gorged ourselves on them. But I had taken the first step and I knew there could be no turning back.

Our second meeting was broken up by the secret police. I expected this—yes, even looked forward to it! I had prepared my sisters by insisting that they file their mandibles until they had transformed them into formidable weapons. But when the confrontation took place, they did not use their mandibles. They simply went limp and allowed themselves to be carried, unprotesting, out of the chamber. I did not go limp and I was not carried out. The head interrogator, whose name is Stahvai, appeared, waved the members of the secret police away and said, "What you are witnessing, Akah-Ki, is simply instinctive behavior." (I was surprised not that he knew my name—members of the secret police know everything!—but that he would use it. He was showing me a great courtesy.) "Your sisters know they have violated their ant natures and are therefore socially disgraced, a condition very close to being no longer alive. Therefore they have gone into a comatose state. They will be carried out of the hill and deposited on the refuse pile, where we place our dead. When they recover they will return, but they will return to work, since that's what they were designed for, and not to listen to your radical rhetoric. Akah-Ki, Akah-Ki! When you first appeared, we were waiting. We recognized you. You did not have a normal birth. You appeared suddenly that morning in Tunnel X27, full grown, in a flash of blinding light. We were there, hovering in the shadows, waiting."

Then I realized that Stah-vai was a sterile sister himself, for all members of the secret police are recruited from the soldier caste, and soldiers are workers. "Why don't you throw away your arm band and join us?" I asked. "With ants such as yourself marching beside us, we could transform this dreary hill into a celestial city."

"I do as I have been instructed to do," Stah-vai replied.

"But my instructions come from a higher power," I said. "In fact, from the Creator himself."

"As do mine," Stah-vai said, drawing a silken thread from his body and moving forward in order to tie me down with it. "As—do—*mine.*"

Now my visions come on, they come on, they come on: the hill in the morning, silent as a dry waterfall, tunnels laid out with scientific precision, odor trails freshly numbered, floors, walls and ceiling neatly tamped down, the chamber of the Queen recently disinfected (meticulously, meticulously), the Queen herself patiently breeding, covered, as with a living blanket, with pulsating males, deep in a profound sleep which extends unbroken back three million years. Then the earth trembles, vibrates, cracks open, explodes, casting up dust, ant mortar, eggs, pupae, startled males, terrified sisters, and fragments of the Queen. "The Revolution! The Revolution!" There are ants, ants, ants everywhere, blinking in the sunlight, transparent in the licking flames, their bodies transformed, spiritual entities at last, having made the great leap forward, falling down to chant hymns of praise to their new leader who is of course—

Me! *Me*—Akah-Ki the Mighty! Me, sitting on a dais, administering justice, dispensing ant love to those who have earned it and casting all others into the flames, the flames, the most prodigious flames!

BEAR

SISTERS, LET US PRAY. Though to be reincarnated as a
Bear is to suffer a hundred physical indignities every day
of your life, we will not complain, O Lord! Though
sweat, salt, blood, excrement, fleas, flies and rotten fish
plague our lives from birth to death, we will continue to
praise you, Omnipotent Being! Though salmon bones,
dead bees and bristles from the backs of arrogant, swag-
gering lovers (never husbands!) stick in our teeth, we
will not complain, for we know that your will is just, O
Lord! Though our intestines are so extensive that if they

were stretched out full length they would reach to the Great Divide and beyond—and consequently we suffer continually from flatulence, rumbling, grumbling, farting and belching as we plod along over the forest paths— yet we will praise you, for we are wonderfully made.

Though we Bears have never seen you, O Lord, our gross corporeal reality—this greasy mass of graying flesh itself—is proof of your existence. Thank you, thank you! Though hunger bites at our bellies like an alligator gar; though lust nips at our genitals, driving us forward unwillingly to more growling, foul-breathed lovers, more troublesome cubs, more trips on your endless Wheel of Existence (from which, release us in your own good time, O Wise One); though our feet go flat and our thighs grow flabby and our eyes fail us, yet we will continue to cry unto our dying day, "Thank you, thank you, thank you!" This old Bear, this Mother Bear, Sophie the Wise, myself, rises on her splendid golden haunches—for which I offer thanks, O Lord, since you created them!—on this magnificent May morning and roars so that not only this small congregation of Bears but the entire forest can hear, "Thank you, thank you, thank you!"

Consider this freshwater clam, O my sisters. Notice how it appeared miraculously between my paws as soon as I expressed gratitude to the Lord. Consider its roundness, the perfection of its shell, its delicate little nose-tweaking scent, the succulence of its pink and pearly inner part. This is no conjurer's trick, for I am not a

Conjure Bear—though some malicious tongues have wagged it about that I am!—and I would like you to step forward and examine this clam. Now consider this pinyon nut as I crack it apart with my one remaining canine tooth (the others being worn down to the nub, to the spongy gumline.) Consider how it was created by the Lord to satisfy my hunger for a pinyon nut at this very moment, and then praise the Lord. Consider the weight of this rock, which supports me, and the shade of this tree, which cools me, and praise the Lord. Consider the fishes, both large and small, which swim in the stream, and praise the Lord. Consider the diamond motes which sparkle in the white water, and the intricate waxy warrens of the honeycomb, and the sunlight—ah, the sunlight!—as it falls on the scales of the rainbow trout and plumps into ripeness the bumps on the raspberry and touches and tickles your black velvet noses, and then praise the Lord!

And now let us pray for the soul of our Sister Belinda, who departed this life, a victim of the dreadful gastroenteritis, last Wednesday afternoon at four o'clock. Oh yes, I know, Belinda was a skeptic, Belinda was a scoffer, Belinda was deep into cynicism and disbelief. We all heard her say, "The absurdity of such gross creatures aspiring to divinity. Why, it makes me laugh!" Belinda isn't laughing any more. We were there when she boasted, "I'll dance on your graves, you bunch of old fogies!" But Belinda isn't dancing any more. We know Belinda was guilty of most of the minor social sins—hoarding fish heads in her den, getting tipsy on mead in the middle of the afternoon, neglecting her cubs. We know also that she defied the Lord by throwing pine cones at the sky in the middle of a thunderstorm. We heard her cry, "The Lord does not exist! We Bears are the gods, just as in the old time!" But I maintain that her frenzy itself was proof of the Lord's existence, for the Lord permitted it. For the Lord was in the storm—oh yes!—but he was also in the pine cones, and he was in our Sister Belinda too, in her intellect and in her questing soul, that soul now whirling out there beyond Ursa Major on a journey we will all undertake one of these days. Praise the Lord, whose treatment of Sister Belinda proves the ultimate beneficence of His divine will, for his love for Belinda was manifest, and in her rage, in her passion, in her despair, she showed us that she loved Him, too.

Now let the Cubs come forth. Softly, softly, my Cubniks, for there are presences in this tree which must not be disturbed, the presence of the bark, the presence of the bud, the presence of the blossom. But the presences will not disturb us if we do not disturb them. So tread softly and don't whisper, don't giggle, don't cry. Now settle down around me while I tell you about your heritage as Bears. There was a time, my little ones, when we Bears were gods. That is why the word "Bear" is always capitalized even today. We were not merely the favorites of the Lord. We were the Gods themselves. In those remote days we lived in caves deeper than any caves which have ever existed since. Some of them reached into the center of the earth itself. Those caves were darker than death, but we could see perfectly in the dark in those days, an ability which we have since lost, sadly enough. For a few hours after they are born all Cubs can see in the dark, but then that ability passes. "We come from the Light but we live in darkness," as the philosopher Bruno of Bald Mountain said long ago. In those days we Bears had perfect understanding. Our minds were like diamonds. We lived in perfect innocence and a blue radiance, similar to the radiance you can see deep, deep in the sky on a cold winter night, emanated from our bodies. We were graceful in those days, not clumsy as we are now. And we all spoke a common language called Ur-Bear, a language appropriate for gods, not the degenerate dialects we speak now. Ur-Bear was pure music, derived from the music of the spheres. But nowadays no Bears sing. We growl, we grunt, we grumble, but any attempt to make music brings bitter, stinging tears to our eyes. Our epic poems, our songs of celebration, our rollicking drinking ditties have all been lost, alas!

Those were the days of the shadow beings, unformed essences of creatures not yet fully realized, like the fox, the wolf, the hare, the goat. We Bears came into our own before any of the others, a fact which every Cub should think about, for it implies grave responsibilities. These shadow beings were in awe of us, waiting on us hand and foot, always eager to do our bidding. Later they learned to imitate us. But we were the first, yes, we were the first. Those were the days, also, of the glacial demons, spirits of the wind, ice and snow, all barbed tails, fingernails and teeth. But we Bears kept them in line, with a little judicial mauling here, a little public whipping there. Our influence reached as far as the moon, my Cubs, for the sound of our roaring reached to the moon, and where our roaring reached there, *there* did we have dominion! Another force was building beyond the moon, but we knew nothing of that in those days.

Once every thousand years we Bears summoned all the creatures before us to see how they were evolving into their proper forms, out of the shadow-mists of their primordial essences. We felt that it was our duty as Bears to watch over the creatures in their evolution from essence into material form. We called it our "stewardship." One year a new creature appeared at the end of the line, a creature perfect in every part, walking upright, with enormous, restless hands and a brain as big as a muskmelon. We dubbed him "The Ape that Walks like a Bear." He had a double nature. One part of him stood in awe of us—that being the correct attitude for creatures—but the other part wanted to trick us, trip us up, humiliate us, bring us down. This wiry, audacious ape, this moody, frequently bored, petulant monster was a trickster, a clown. But he could be lovable, charming, witty, nimble—all the things which Bears were then but are not now. We kept this creature near us at all times, partly to keep our eye on him, but partly also because he amused us. He brought humor into the world. His double nature made wit possible. And often when he was most cruel, he was most amusing. He made us realize that a bruised butt or a broken bone could be funny. We were ashamed of ourselves, but we roared with laughter. Everything that man has subsequently done was inherent in his double nature. Oh yes, I know, but we had a weakness for man, and it touches our hearts to see what he's become.

Then we Bears fell. One morning we woke to find that the radiance was gone from our bodies. We heard no morning hymns from the hillsides. We stood at the entrances to our caves, expecting the traditional gestures of respect and reverence, but it wasn't to be. Every insect which had been created up to that time flew over us, but not a single one dipped his wing. The ungulates down on the prairie—the bison, the musk ox, the horse—went in grazing. We Bears roared in unison, the greatest roar that has ever been roared in the history of the world, but they only glanced up briefly, looked at us blankly, and then returned to their grazing. Man sat on a rock, eating berries and grinning at us. One thought formed in his mind and we could read it, since it was written in the expression on his face. (We could no longer see beyond that face into the melon brain behind, however.) That thought was, "I told you so!" But man had never told us anything, of course. And we knew that he did not possess the power of prophecy. How had he known that this would happen?

It was then that we saw man's mate for the first time, sitting in the shadow of the rock, heavy with child, totally self-absorbed, her eyes half closed, her lips pressed into a mystical, other-worldly smile. Man's mate was the only creature ever to escape our stewardship entirely. We were astounded. But we had no time to think about her. Already the cries were going up, "We have fallen! We have fallen! What are we supposed to do now?"

Well, we did what any creatures would do under the circumstances. We fell on our knees, wept and prayed. Prayed to whom? We didn't know. Until then we Bears had been prayed to by others. Praying to something higher than a Bear was a new experience. Then we fasted, going without food for longer than we thought possible. Fasting was another new experience. And we rubbed ashes, dung and nettles into our magnificent furry flesh—magnificent, yes, but not in the same way! But it was all to no avail. It was then that the great questions began to be asked. "Why did we fall?" And, "What did we do to warrant such punishment?"

Here then are the five traditional answers. First, Heliogabalus of Kush. "You fell because you ate green beans, which goes against the Lord's decree forbidding the ingestion of green beans." Second, Melius of Macedonia. "You fell because your sign, Ursa Major, shifted its position in the night sky, moving closer to the sun and away from the moon, the moon looking favorably upon Bears, the sun on something else." Third, "You fell because some other creature took over the means of production." I forget who said that. Fourth, Rufus of Greenwich, "You fell because all things fall. Test it with a rock. Toss it in the air and watch it fall. It's universal law." And finally, Denis of Dunstan. "Man did it." Yes, perhaps he did. But how? We Bears have never been able to find out.

So I say that it is and will remain a sacred mystery. Allow yourselves to rest in the sacred mystery, my cubs, never seeking ultimate answers—there may be none— but content always to contemplate what is ultimately unknowable, the Lord above, whom we have never seen. This is all a bit much for cubs. This is all a bit much for me! When my spirit falls through space, impelled on its way by some power higher than my own; when my next incarnation appears on the horizon, like an island looming up in the distance in the middle of a great lake, as we swim toward it, drowning as we swim; when the Lord looks down, pats the back of my paw and says, "Good Bear! Well done!"; then and only then will I know the answers to the questions which plague us from conception to extinction.

Now Sister Ursula will pass among you with a reed basket. I'm sure there will be generous contributions this morning. Afterwards there are honeycakes for the Cubs and, for you adult Bears, fat, blue-backed grubs, gathered just this morning from a damp place under a decaying log just above Badger Creek. Ah, I can see the saliva forming on your lips right now. So eat, eat, my Sisters! Eat and be joyful. Thank you thank you thank you.

COW

As you can see, my friends, I am a cow. My owner, Mr. Miller, calls me "Thelma." He don't know it, but "Thelma" was my name in my other lifetime too—Thelma R. (for Rita) Hodge of near-Joplin, Missouri. Maiden name—Hubbard, same as the squash. I married John Hodge when I was sixteen and we had eleven kids —Duane, Melanie, Dulcie, Cass, Joan, Tessie, Liz, Ellwood (that was born with the hare lip), Harry, Bud and Bo, my twins. And I always knew I'd come back as a cow. I just never knew what kind I'd be. Well, I'm a

Holstein and bein' a Holstein suits me just fine. Layin' out here in the shade of this peachleaf willow, dappled all over with shadows, my black and white coat all shiny and smooth, y'know—why I must look like a six hundred pound mocha milkshake, ho, ho! Oh yes, I always knew. We Hubbards and Hodges, we was hardshell Baptists, but I never did believe in that Baptist heaven and hell. I was more like one of them heathen Hindus than any Baptist you'll ever meet. (Course I never let on.) My idea of heaven was a big meadow just like this one, full of deep, sweet grass—grass so green it makes a body's eyes brim over to look at it—with a nice little prairie creek runnin' along below all sparkly and blue. You can see the creek if you raise your head up a little bit above the grass. And my hell? Well, I guess my hell was the slaughter house, but why talk about that on a nice summer afternoon like this one? We Hodges lived on a six hundred acre farm ten miles from Joplin, so I was around animals all the time, but none ever caught my fancy the way them cows did. I used to watch 'em all the time. There's somethin' so peaceful and happy and solid and good about a cow! Cows don't hardly ever complain. Since I been out here, which is about two years now, I ain't heard hardly one cross or crotchety word. Mostly we cows just like to lay out here, chewin' our cuds—which, by the by, has a greeny, grayish taste, kind of like cottage cheese when it's begun to turn sour—swishing our tails at flies, licking at each other with our big soft leathery tongues and, oh! just

24

dreamin' our lifetimes away! Believe you me, it is just heavenly being a cow. Yes, I was a Baptist, and I was buried with the Holy Bible, but it was a book I never did get around to reading. I kept it around for show, y' know, but it never did interest me much. My Holy Bibles was all out in the barn, and sometimes I'd sneak out there on a night when there was a full moon and touch them cows on their flanks and udders and look deep, deep in their gentle, sleepy eyes, and *I* knew, and *they* knew! And that was always enough for me, Thelma R. Hodge of near-Joplin, Missouri.

Yes, I always knew. Because there was other signs too, of course. I used to see them bumper stickers on the cars and trucks, y'know—like "Milk the Udder Cola!"—and I'd laugh right out loud every time, ho, ho! There weren't no other bumper stickers ever made me laugh right out like that. I only noticed them ones that mentioned milk. One time my sister Callie, the one that suffered so from all those allergies, went to New Mexico to escape the ragweed, and she sent me this funny card that showed a cow stepping on its udder, and under the picture it said, "Some days it just don't pay to get up in the morning!" Well, I laughed till I cried. Kept that card in my kitchen for years, on the nick-nack shelf next to the wall clock. It tickled me so! (Though stepping on your udder can be very painful, you bet.) Now I can see that you are thinking, remembering I said I had eleven kids, "If it don't pay to get up in the morning, it sure as shootin' didn't pay that Thelma Hodge to lay down at night!" But every single one of them kids was wanted and every single one was loved. All of 'em is growed up now and havin' kids of their own (except for my twins, who never will get married, I guess), and all their kids is loved too. There's a sight more love in this world to-day 'cause Thelma R. Hodge lived in it for 58 years. They had one of them family reunions for me on my 57th birthday—had they guessed how soon that heart condition would do their old Maw in?—and I counted 87 Hodges, and there's been two or three more since then, glory hallelujah! Y'know, I never could stand the thought of taking a kid off milk. It was like death to me, not havin' a child at my breast. So before the time come to wean him, I'd make sure I had another on the way. Oh there ain't nothin' more deep-down soul satis-fyin' than giving sustenance to a child!

Yes, sustenance, nourishment, food, food, food! Be-cause if you ain't eatin', if you off your feed, as they say, you ain't livin'! And did we Hodges ever love to eat! Why, I stuffed my kids till their belly buttons squeaked and till I heard that squeak I just kept on stuffin'. "I ain't heard that little squeak yet," I'd say, and then I'd shovel in some more. And, oh Lord, them Sunday dinners! Shepherd's pie, chicken casserole, baked ham with brown sugar glaze, pot roast in my own special gravy, pork chops with apple rings, candied sweet potatoes, baked squash, macaroni and cheese, corn fritters, baked beans, hominy grits, gumbo, country fried tomatoes, cornmeal biscuits with strawberry jam, Southern fried chicken, cornedbeef hash, catfish, pig's knuckles, brains, watermelon pickles, slaw, turnip greens, cucumbers in vinegar custards frankfurters chocolate cake noodles goulash Jello bananacream pieshrimp capon with gibletgravygingerbread whippedcreambraisedvenisonkidneys mushroomsprunewhippiccalilli zucchini friedokra stewappleturnovertomato soup potatopancakespietongue calfsliversauteed sweetbreadscreamedchipbeef tripe hashbrownshotrolls orange cupcakes icecreambroiledsteaks mush "Oh, I ain't heard that little squeaksqueak-squeakin' sound yet," I'd holler. "I ain't heard that squeak-squeak-squeakin' sound!" Boiledbrisket shortribs honeycreampeachpie hamroll sauerbratenwatercress sauerkrautmeatloaf Salisbury steak pork tenderloin Welshrabbitchickenalakingtunacasserole oatmealcookiesSquee Pancakes withblue berriesSquee RolledstuffedfudgebrowniesSqueeSquee "I'm listenin' but I ain't hearin' nothin'!" I'd say. Sweettaterpuffpickledbeefheartbrownbettypeachcobblerkohlrabi Squee rumfruitrutabaga Squee Squee Squee "I'm listenin' but I ain't a'hearin' nothin'!" Cucumber croquettescreamcheeseSqueezeSqueeze Grahamcrackerpie I! I! Nonono! No mo', Maw! Cain't eat no mo', Maw! Maw Maw Maw! "You sayin' 'More more more,' chile?" No no no! CreampuffsBlackbottompieChocolatepeanut balls Date 'n pecanlogsKriskringlesMarshmallowsMolassescookiesJellyballsRaspberrycrumblesPeanutbutter-

coconutbrowniesPineapple UpsidedowncakeRaspber-
ryjellyrollohohohNonono! Squeesquee squee squeeeeee
SQUEE—EE—EE—EEK!

"Ah, there she is now. OK. You can quit."

As Thelma Hodge I had only one stomach. As Thelma the Cow I got four, so I reckon I come out ahead
this trip, ho, ho!

But oh, how I do miss them good old times! Every
Saturday John and me, we'd toss them kids in the back
of the pickup and take off for town, laughin' and singin'
all the way, just so durned happy to be alive! We'd get
the kids to do "Ole Mack Donald's Farm" and they'd
oink and quack and bow wow and baa baa and meow
and moo, and ever' livin' soul in Joplin knew the Hodges was headin' for town. Horses and pigs and sheep and
goats'd stampede across the fields and folks'd lock their
doors and run for their storm cellars, yellin', "Them
Hodges is a'comin'! Them Hodges is a'comin'!" And it
was "Tornado Alert" every Saturday when we drove to
town. My, you could hear us for miles. And wasn't it
glorious! And then them stores! How I did love them
big stores— *Woolco, K-Mart, Sears, Penney's, Monkey
Ward's*. Them clerks'd turn whiter'n a sheet, watching
me and my kids mosey up and down the aisles. They
was afraid we'd break somethin' or steal some of their
merchandise. But none of my kids never stole nothin'
from no store! Oh, how I'd love to go back as a human
being and shop in them wonderful stores again. But the
only thing worser'n a bull in a china shop is a Holstein

28

cow in a *K-Mart*. Can't you just see me in the shape I'm in now, marchin' up and down them aisles, a flowered kerchief on my horns, buttin' my shopping cart along with my black and white forehead? Ho, ho! Well, about six o'clock we'd go to one of them buffet places—you know, "All You Can Eat for $1.98!" "Kids Half Price!" And I'd turn those kids loose sayin', "OK. Go drive 'em outta business!" And them kids would strip that table like a mess of locusts stripping an alfalfa field. And when we'd stuffed ourselves fit to bust, we'd take in a movie. How I did love them "Ma and Pa Kettle" pictures. Seen every last one of 'em twice over, and then three or four more times on the TV back home. Oh, I knowed about folks in town callin' us "The Kettles" behind our backs and their kids makin' my kids miserable at the new consolidated school, but I used to say, "Never you mind, honeypots. Them folks is just jealous 'cause they envies the love we has for one another." It was all hardest on l'il Ellwood 'cause he had that there hare lip and never was too good in school. But I'd dry his tears and say, "Never you mind, sweetheart. You is loved, and that's all that matters." Sometimes I see Miller's son comin' down through the pasture and he has that whitish hair just like Ellwood had, and that scared, rabbity look too (I swear Ellwood was a rabbit before he was mine), and I call out, "Ellie, Ellie, my love! Come over here and sit down by your Maw." But I ain't "Maw" no more. And my heart breaks to see him passin' so close and me not able to hold him and pat his cheek and kiss his tears

29

away like in the old days. And he ain't even Ellwood. I think he's called "Calvin" or something like that. Once a mother, always a mother, even when she's a cow.

I had a dream the other night, for cows dream just like humans do, and in that dream I was Thelma R. Hodge again, layin' in my bed back home. I was alone, John bein' away at one of those NFO meetin's in Kansas City, and the terrible anxiety of bein' alone weighed on me. Y' know how it is, waking up alone when you're used to havin' someone right there next to you. Well, I heard one of my kids cry out from a room down the hall, "Hey, Maw! Come quick. We needs y'." And I remembered that some of 'em was down with the croup and I pulled myself out of bed to go to 'em. But I couldn't hardly move myself off that bed. I seemed to weigh a ton or more. When my feet hit the floor, I kinda slipped and slid, as if I'd got a new set of legs and hadn't learned to walk on 'em yet. "Hold on," I hollered. "I'm a'comin'. I'm a'comin'." But I couldn't really make a single sound. The noises just stuck in my throat, like air bubbles in a tube. And when I finally got to the threshold and tried to get through the door, why I got stuck! My sides just wouldn't fit through, no matter which way I turned. I could still hear my kids callin' out, "Maw, come quick!" And I could see down that long dark hall, with the light comin' out from under the door where their room was, but I couldn't get through—*nohow! noway!* I pushed and shoved and heaved till the skin on my hips broke and blood run down my legs, but I jus' couldn't get through. My belly got heavier and heavier and my thighs blew up till they was twice their natural size, but still I kept tryin' to get through, cryin' out, though no one could hear me, "I'm a'comin'! I'm a'comin'! Hold on, I'm a'comin' to y'." Then I broke into a million pieces and woke up in my stall, those pieces rearranging themselves into the cow you see before you now. Just thinkin' about that dream makes my skin all trembly (look at it!) and it ain't from those pesky flies landin' on it neither. I hope I never have another dream like that as long as I live.

But as I ease myself up, as I'm doin' now, to follow the other cows in for the milkin', it bein' about five o'clock I'd guess, I always say to myself, "No regrets, Thelma! No regrets." Because life is its own reward and I lived it and I loved it. Now, if you will excuse me, I gotta be moo-ovin' along because du-ooty calls.

FOX

YOU'RE ABSOLUTELY RIGHT, OF COURSE. No fox would ever venture out at night without his mask and his magic talisman. That would be to invite disaster. Fox law states unequivocally, "No mask, no talisman, no night journey." This is my mask; this is my talisman. I'll let you examine them in more detail in a moment. But first, you're a goose, aren't you? Your letter from the newspaper made no mention of that fact. I admit, I'm surprised. No, astonished! Tell me, doesn't it frighten you—given the reputation of foxes, I mean—finding yourself alone and unprotected in a fox's den? It doesn't? Oh. By the way, would you like a glass of California pinot chardonnay? It's quite good, really. Oh, you don't drink? Well, perhaps some mineral water then? I always have a glass or two of good wine before dinner. It clears the palate as it whets the appetite. The cleansing effect of this particular wine is extraordinary and it has a delicate piquancy which is absolutely divine. And while I'm on the subject of excellence in wine, let me add something about excellence in women. You are the most attractive female goose I've seen in years, my dear. Yes, you are. Now that self-deprecating modesty will get you nowhere here. Your qualities illuminate the room. And I especially admire your courage—maintaining your calm demeanor in the presence of a fox who has the reputation of being—how can I put it? Oh, more than a little experienced with women. Hmm? And your concern for your newspaper is certainly commendable. Of course I'll help you in any way I can. I was honestly touched by the last sentence of your letter. "A newspaper stands or falls by the accuracy of its reporting." So you came directly to the source. You took the risk. Ah, that every reporter possessed that kind of courage! You have nerves of steel, my dear, a quality rare in any creature, but especially rare in a female goose.

I published a newspaper myself before I went into politics, you know. You do know? Ah, you've done research on me, of course. And now that I'm out of office, now that I'm no longer in politics, now that I've been so

abruptly, so arbitrarily and so unfairly thrown out...!
But sit over here, please. The sofa is so much more comfortable. Try some of these canapes—avocado, a little lemon juice, pitted olives. Oh, you *are* a vegetarian! You see, I guessed. So many creatures are into that now. I suppose you meditate and do yoga, too? And jog every morning? A ferret ward heeler said once, "The sight of a goose jogging would make the angels weep!" But not a bit of it, my dear. Not a bit of it. Motion is beauty. Movement is grace. Any movement, any motion. But all this clean living! This sudden penchant for asceticism, for morality! It's always the same, isn't it? When you get a Reform Candidate in, moral uplift and self denial follow. As you know, it wasn't that way before the last election, before I was removed from office, along with my brothers. But, think about it! A Reformist who stuffs ballot boxes, who resorts to extortion, to intimidation...! The irony of it makes my teeth tingle! But why go into a rage? All in a day's work, as they say. Here, let me adjust the light so that it doesn't shine directly into your eyes. There, that's better, isn't it?

I'm sure you've heard the old saying, "Beware the fox who wears a smiling mask?" Well, as you can see from my mask, which has a grave almost sullen expression, there's nothing to fear from me. This is the mask for lawyers, counselors, administrators and, as the old saying puts it, "The fox whose lips have brushed the ear of the king." This mask was owned originally by William Cecil, the first Baron Burghley, adviser to Queen

Elizabeth the First. It's been in my family since 1598. As the eldest son, I inherited it when I reached my majority in. . . . But you already know when I came of age, don't you, Greta? It is "Greta," isn't it? Yes, you have that air of mystery about you, that Garbo quality. The line of your throat—so pure, so white!—when you throw your head back and laugh like that, is so very exciting. Your parents named you wisely. Often, when they name us, our parents surprise us with their insights. They seem to see so deeply into our inner natures. My name—Sardonicus—was given to me because I emerged from the womb wearing a crooked grin. My middle name, Russel, refers to the redness in my coat. Observe how your webbed foot shows up against my rich, blood-red fur—black against red, as with playing cards. Do you see any mystical significance in the colors? Oh, you aren't into the mysticism of color yet. A pity. But perhaps it will come to you later. Foxes have always been active in religious organizations, you know. Many Roman Catholic cardinals have been reincarnated as foxes. And you are probably not aware of this, but the souls of Niccolo Machiavelli, Sir Walter Raleigh and Benjamin Disraeli passed immediately into the bodies of foxes as soon as they expired. Each time the soul of a famous person passes into the body of a fox, we foxes are rewarded in a special way, though I can't tell you how, since all foxes take a sacred oath never to reveal that. We almost finessed the soul of the poet Rimbaud, but it finally went into the body of a Malaysian

35

civet cat instead. If Rimbaud had died at sixteen, we'd have had him, for at the age of sixteen Rimbaud was pure fox.We've lost several poets to the cat family—Poe, Baudelaire, Villon. I have never understood why this should be so.

Here, hold my mask in your wing, Greta. Now you are probably the only goose in history to hold a fox's mask in her lily-white wing. Nervous? No? Calm as can be! Oh, Greta, what a treasure you are! But observe the construction of the mask. As you can see, it's made from strips of laminated wood—tradition says, English walnut—reinforced on the inside with gutta-percha. The gutta-percha was added during the 19th Century, about the time of the Franco-Prussian War. The lower part of the mask is hinged, so that the mouth can open and close. The hinge must be oiled on our High Holy Days. I cannot reveal to you the ingredients of the oil we use, sorry. I told you that this was the mask of foxes who give counsel to kings, so I need not belabor the rather obvious symbolism of the moving mouth. Notice the intricate little steel spring between the eyelids. The eyes move from side to side, very slyly, as the lids go up and down. Listen to the "ping" the spring makes when I release it—pure music, pure poetry, designed to charm the ear of anyone who happens to be in power at the moment. Richelieu put himself to sleep every night of his life thinking of the "ping" in this little steel spring. It has such a soothing sound, doesn't it? A hypnotic quality! Lean closer, little goose. You're

36

missing the full effect of it. *Ping*! He, he! *Ping, ping*! It's
so good to hear you laugh, to know you're loosening up
a bit! And why not? I'm not your editor, you know. I'm
not going to give you a dressing-down for failing to get
a story in on time. Ah, but the mask, the mask! This
reddish color is cochineal, a scarlet dye made from the
bodies of certain South American insects. Only the female of the species can give us this dye and over a million of them were sacrificed for this one mask alone. The
color signifies "fox." Baron Burghley had a red face,
which his enemies attributed to drink or venereal dis-
ease, but it was simply the "fox" showing through. As
they say, "In the flushed face, the fox we trace." The
odor—that musky, penetrating, bone-chilling odor?
That is incense, the incense used in all our ceremonies—
initiation, marriage, funeral. What you're sniffing there
so delicately, so fastidiously, is four hundred years of
ritual, blood ritual, sperm ritual, moon ritual. That's po-
tent magic—the smell of death and rebirth, lust, copula-
tion, gestation, murder, sacrifice. Heady stuff! That's
why your beak is quivering now. That's why your
feathers are ever-so-slightly ruffled. You geese have no
equivalent of this. What! You say that Force that drives
you across the sky during your migrations? Did I hear
you correctly? You must be joking. Your magic is white
magic, the magic of clouds, of air, of thin reeds singing
on banksides, of sunlight warming the delicate casings
of the eggs in your ephemeral nests. Our magic is dark
red, the magic of blood—heavy, deep, timeless, like a

37

pool at the very bottom of a cave. Your magic is a day-time magic and you tremble in terror when it deserts you immediately after sunset. But our magic is the magic of four A.M., of the hunt, the kill! Our magic involves the ecstacy of yellow eye, ravening tooth, the hot dry rage in the back of the throat as we leap forward out of our cover for the kill!

Ah, but I'm getting carried away. Greta, you are even more attractive when you blanch, did you know that? The purity of your whiteness! You have a soul of purest snow—so unlike my own, I'm afraid, which has been soiled by so many sins. We are opposites, little one, and opposites attract. It's fate, our coming together like this. If I turn my head away, forgive me, it's because, given my canine nature, I can't help seeing your cloud-white feathers streaked with blood. I can't help it. I was born this way. I'm pure fox, after all. Oh, yes, the mask! Well, the hairs around the lips are from Raleigh's beard. They appeared on the face of the mask a second after he was beheaded in 1618. The mask weighs four pounds. Each eye socket is two and a half inches in diameter. From crown to chin, the mask measures nine inches exactly. The teeth—are real.

That noise you hear? It's the steel door opening into the inner chamber. My brothers are coming in for supper. I'd like you to meet them. As you can see, they are the cream of the fox line. Cornelius, Gonzalo, Rex, Simonides, Alexas, Saturninus, Alcibiades—I'd like you to meet Greta, who's here to do an in-depth interview with us for the paper. What do you think of my brothers' Renaissance costumes, Greta? For a fox, it is always the High Renaissance, century after century. Have you ever seen more gorgeous ruffs, jerkins, peascod doublets? Yes, they reek! They reek wonderfully! And, yes, their capes are streaked with blood! Magnificent! How they do bring in the fear that rides on the cold evening air!

Has it been accomplished then, my brothers? Is what I read in your eyes correct? Yes, yes? Well, Greta, I'll give you the news before your paper prints it. Your Reformist has been—how can I put this, he, he!—removed from office, permanently. I feel like doing a little dance now! We've won, we've won! Clasp hands, my brothers! Our candidate, that whippet, that faggot whippet whom we can control, will replace that hypocritical, overbearing, self righteous . . . ! Is he really dead? This puts an even finer edge on what was already a wonderful evening.

You see, Greta, political parties exist to perpetuate political games. Reform movements, elections, laws— all window dressing! Speaking of dressing! But no, even *I* couldn't be that indelicate. You say you want to examine the talismans? All right, I see no reason why I can't oblige you. As your keen eye has detected, each of my brothers is wearing his talisman around his neck. When I give the signal, each will demonstrate his talisman for you. Each talisman is made of carved bone and each is in the shape of a phallus. The glans penis is made of ebony, a wood sacred to the spirits of the night. Notice the contrast between the white of the polished bone and the ebony. This symbolizes life and death. Life grows out of death and death follows life. Spirit grows out of flesh, as the confused aspirations of the soul grow out of the absolute certainties of blood and sperm. So now, my brothers, push the buttons at the base of your talismans revealing—why, seven knives, my dear! *Knives!* Of course. What did you expect, marshmallows? And that sound you hear coming from the kitchen—the clashing of cutlery, the rattling of a roasting pan! What did you expect to hear in a fox's den at suppertime? Someone playing Chopin, reciting the poetry of Ella Wheeler Wilcox, dancing the gavotte? Come come, sweetheart, you wanted this. You wouldn't have come here if you hadn't wanted this. You know and I know that this was all predicated in the vapid sexual passions of your dimwitted parents, in the egg which housed you, in the illusions which nourished and sustained you through your protected childhood, in the insipid prayers you offered up to your gods of water and mist and swamp grass. Call on them now! See how much good it will do you. Oh, don't flutter that way, Greta, my love. It excites us so. Have pity on our poor throbbing glands. Listen, I was aware of your latent death wish as soon as you stepped over the threshold. Rex, what does the Sacred Book tell us to do about death wishes? Why, satisfy them, of course! But think of it this way, Greta. You are about to participate in a ceremony ordained by the Creator Himself—the ritual rape, murder and dismemberment of a

40

foolish goose by a group of foxes following the earliest of His commands, that is, "Thou shalt honor thy instincts above all else, for they came first as the foundation for all things." By the way, Saturninus, do try some of that pinot chardonnay. It's really excellent. Greta, Greta, I'm bending close not to bite you, though that will come in time, but to offer you some words of wisdom and perhaps also of consolation. It's a quotation from Holderlin. "Where danger is, there is salvation also." You have seen your salvation. We are here before you. Now give me your throat. A kiss, yes, a mere kiss! We're in no hurry. It has been preordained that this ceremony will not end until sunrise.

Are you ready, O my brothers?

GNAT

I WAS NEVER NOTHING. Before time was, I existed as an idea in the divine mind, as a collection of radiant atoms emanating from cosmic consciousness. But after my millionth death and rebirth, I woke to find myself swimming in seemingly endless circles of pure white light, surrounded by billions of my brothers and sisters, all of whom were singing "Hish-y-shirini" (which can be translated into English as "ecstacy in adoration," though that does not convey the quality of it), and all of whom were being menaced and devoured by that selfsame white light. Then I realized that I had been reincarnated as a gnat and I was filled with a very great joy, for special things have been promised to gnats, who qualify as creatures who constitute "the very least of these." The light crackled with the terror of birth and violent death, for as billions died, billions more were born, and all within split (no, within shattered!) megaseconds of timeless time so infinitely small no human chronometer could ever have measured it. Then I understood the meaning of "entering in at the narrow gate," but of course there was no gate, only a slight increase in the intensity of the light down at the center of the vortex toward which we were all being drawn. I knew that I was being spared momentarily (if the word "momentarily" can have any meaning in this context), in order to witness a great truth and to pass that truth on to posterity. (Though a thousand generations of my "posterity" were expiring all around me, as I paused there, drawn toward death but tied to life by some force I did not fully understand.) I know you've seen insects—moths, midges, who knows what—crowding around streetlights on summer nights, knocking each other aside in their eagerness to thrust their frail, foolish bodies into the light. They too are truth seekers, but the only truth they uncover is a truth already inherent in the molecular structure of every insect, namely, that we were created in order to be zapped in the light. But my truth was not like theirs. My cells told me, "For you, and for you alone, Nikki, there is no death, and what lies at the center of the vortex is eternal life." Why had I been chosen? I didn't know. Perhaps I had performed heroic actions in some previous existence. (It's so hard to remember previous existences when you're a gnat. You have so little time for reflection.) Perhaps I'd been an Achilles, a Hercules, a Jason. But as soon as I knew that my fate was different from that of the others, I was filled with bliss, and I had a vision of a meadow of asphodel watched over by a beaming, benevolent sun god, and I knew that I had been granted a glimpse of the heaven reserved for good insects. I experienced that special peace that passeth understanding and I knew that the spirit of God moved in my tiny body (for the Creator is incarnate in the smallest of things) and that I had been singled out as his special gnat to illustrate some great, universal truth. "Zizi-nez! Zizi-nez!" I cried (which means both "I love you" and "I thank you.") "For the truth which I am about to illustrate—Zizi-nez! Zizi-nez!"

Then I heard God's voice cry, "Neti, neti!" ("Not this, not this!"), and I knew that each insect around me had been granted the same vision as myself (for we insects are never separate, we are never alone, we possess a collective ego after all), and in the full realization of my self-deception I fell in flaming terror toward Absolute Truth.

HEN

An immortal spirit, perceiving that it was about to be thrust into some corporeal form, humbled itself and prayed. "Dear Lord, I care not what the impending form might be—rat, weasel, whale, ape, I'm indifferent —but please, if you value justice, as you say you do, don't thrust me into the body of a hen again. If you grant me this request, I'll praise your munificence with every cell in the body of whatever creature I happen to inhabit as long as that creature shall live. But you have condemned me to a hen a hundred times now and I simply cannot bear it any more. So please, Lord, anything but a hen!" The spirit then fell into the most profound of sleeps, a sleep deeper than any we mortals can imagine, and woke to find itself firmly encased in the well-padded body of a hen. A moment after waking, the spirit utilized its new senses. Smell—chicken shit. Sounds—a nervous, rapid cackling, the same excruciating treble vibrato it remembered from other incarnations. Taste—bran. Touch—the tenuous security of a spattered perch.

"I'm a hen again," the spirit thought. "Henceforth I'll be known as 'Hen.'" Then, hiding her head under her wing, she cursed God in secret and wished she could die.

As all hens know, there is nothing new under the sun. When Hen finally overcame her depression and sauntered forth into the yard, she heard the other hens debating the same philosophical questions they'd been debating for years.

"Are these substances on the ground seeds or are they shadows," a hen named Emma asked. "Some maintain that they are shadows, while others insist that they are seeds. Still others say that they are both, since it sometimes seems that they are seeds in the morning when the farmer's wife comes through, and shadows in the afternoon. Is it merely a matter of perception or do these objects have an objective reality independent of our senses? If they are merely shadows, we cannot eat them, and if they are not sustenance, why are we concerned with them?"

A blossoming pear tree hung over the yard and Hen could see, simply by glancing up, that they were arguing about the shadows of the blossoms on the boughs. But she also knew it would do no good to tell them so. Hens are fixated on philosophical questions which they cannot answer. Hen knew also that they would conclude by forming a committee to investigate the problem further, since hens love committee meetings, and this is what they did. "I think we should form an *ad hoc* committee to investigate the problem further," one of them cried. "*Ad hoc, ad hoc!*"

"*Ad hoc,*" the others replied. And it was done.

Hen looked down at her body for the first time in this her most recent incarnation and knew total despair. Breast bone, wish bone, alligator skin pipestem legs, whisk broom wings good only for flapping in the dust —no doubt about it, Hen was hen, again! She shrieked in grief at her situation and it clicked from her throat with a sound like a spinning ratchet wheel. "Why, why, why?" she cried. *Click, click, click!* It was at that moment that Hen decided to do away with herself and set out to find the fox. The only way out of this was the death of the body, and the fox had been programmed to bring that about.

Hen found him without any difficulty, and it was the same scruffy old fox she'd known in her previous lifetime. His name was Bill. "My dear, I'm so bored," Bill said to Hen, looking up from the grass where he was lying half-hidden. "I mean, it's always the same story. I catch the cock by the throat and carry him off. Then everybody and his brother chases me. The cock talks me into opening my mouth to shout back at them, at which point I lose my lunch. The trouble is, there's never any variety! Know what I mean?"

"I know where you're at," Hen replied, stepping enticingly between his extended forepaws. "Life is a bore."

The fox, being a creature of instinct, began to salivate. His teeth glistened like a tray of jewels. A quivering bark began to rise from the cherry red depths of his throat. Hen trembled, for she felt that death was near. She could smell it and the odor was exciting—musky and slightly saline. She placed her neck in the jaws of death just to make the inevitable end easier. But the jaws did not clamp shut. "I'm ready, Bill," she said, closing her eyes. "What are you waiting for?"

The fox did not reply.

Hen withdrew her neck and peered up at him inquisitively, in a way that only hens can peer. He seemed to have been turned to stone. Yes, this fox, who had been the archway through which so many hens had flapped forth into a happier world, had been immobilized. Hen recognized the hand of God in this. Who except God could have frozen poor old Bill into this position? "Hmm. This suicide thing isn't going to be as easy as I thought it would be," Hen said. Then she walked away, turning her back on the astonished fox, who remained there on his tussock of grass, mouth open, eyes popping,

48

teeth gleaming, one drop of saliva glistening on his lower lip.

Each afternoon an hour before sundown Cock presided over vespers for the assembled hens. "Oh, Lord," the hens chanted. "Make us fat and fertile and allow us to live forever just as we are now—your humble hens, Greta, Emma, Hilda, Francine, Rita, Isadora!" And Hen prayed with them, knowing Cock would be angry with her if she refused to join in. But in her heart she recited another prayer. "Dear God, I want only to be released from forms, from horizontals, from verticles, from roosts, from chopping blocks, from egg cartons, from chicken wire fences. Free me now from my light meat and my dark, from my lice-ridden feathers, from this assembly line of an ovarian system which simply serves to perpetuate more useless forms on this sad earth!"

Thunder rumbled over the blossoming pear tree. They all looked up. Then Sybil, a Plymouth Rock with second sight, became highly excited and said, "Yes, yes, my sisters, God has spoken to us. But for some strange reason, the only word he spoke was, 'No!'"

Fall came, followed by winter. Greta, Emma, Hilda all vanished one by one, to be killed, dressed, roasted, broiled or stewed to grace some farmer's table at a Sunday dinner. Only Hen remained, in spite of all her attempts to destroy herself. During the harvest, she threw herself into the threshing machine, but it spit her out unharmed. Again, she climbed to the top of the barn and jumped off the roof, but a breeze caught her halfway down, carried her to the ground and gently cushioned her fall. She tried to drown herself in the water trough, as so many melancholy hens had done before her, but the waters parted like the Red Sea and she merely banged her head on the wet wood at the bottom. "My identity is a burden to me," she thought. "But I carry it around with me like the comb on my head. There's no way I can dispose of it."

A whole new generation of hens appeared and began to debate the same philosophical questions the previous generation had debated, with no more success than their forebears had had. "Are these objects we perceive seeds or shadows?" a Rhode Island Red named Esther asked. "Peck, peck! Well, that was a seed, obviously. But that object over there! Tell me, is that a seed or is it a shadow?"

Exasperated beyond endurance, Hen cried out, "You stupid hens! Can't you see how foolish you are? Don't you understand what God has done to you? Can't you see how he designed you this way for a purpose? He knew you needed something to occupy your empty heads from the egg to the chopping block, so He programmed you to ask these stupid questions over and over, generation after generation. But he made it an absolute certainty that you would never, never penetrate to the truth!"

"Oh my!" the other hens cried in unison. "Oh my, oh my!" Then one of them ran for Cock, who mounted Hen immediately, this being the only remedy they knew for attacks of the vapors like this one. As the feathering commenced, Hen cried, "Cock, you know nothing about the real, the true, the inner Hen!"

"No, and I could care less," answered Cock, and he continued with his conjugal duty like the good bourgeois rooster that he was. "There! That should settle you down for a while," he said, after he had finished. Then he strutted back across the yard, chuckling to himself.

But it settled nothing, for Hen's condition grew worse. She began to have visions and she developed the conviction that she had a separate existence somewhere else and lived in a radiant body which was not the body of a hen in some distant world. She knew that in that world she was called Hen Transformed and she made the mistake of telling the other hens about it.

"This other body of yours," one of them said spitefully. "What's it like? Like a duck's? Or maybe it's like a pigeon's. Ha, ha, ha!"

"Or a crow's!" cried a second. "Yuck, yuck!"

They all laughed at her, but she refused to admit that she was deluded. One night she got a message from Somewhere Else. It rocked her off her perch and onto the floor of the henhouse. "Avoid the ovoid," the voice cried. "Avoid the ovoid."

"But how can I possibly avoid the ovoid?" she asked. "I'm a hen! My whole world is centered around the ovoid. My body was designed to produce ovoids. Why did God make me a hen if he wanted me to avoid the ovoid?"

"Nevertheless, avoid the ovoid," the voice said again. Then it tuned out. Hen came to herself to see the other hens looking down at her from their perches, clucking in a concerned manner. Some showed pity, others consternation; but most seemed simply bewildered.

"No one here understands me," Hen thought, and she determined at that moment to leave the flock forever. That morning, at sunrise, she departed, imagining that she would find some definitive answers in the world outside.

Hen wandered through the world for a long time, never growing any older, never in danger of death. During her wanderings she observed an astonishing variety of forms—from the slick black water beetle to the draft horse—but never did any of these forms seem purposeful in any transcendent sense. In all the natural world, she was the only creature who believed she had two forms, led two lives, had two destinies. "Your idea about duality is an absurdity," a Jersey cow told her. "What would any creature want with two bodies? Why, I have enough to do to stuff the one I've been given!"

"There's more to life than stuffing," Hen replied.

"You are one crazy hen," the cow said. "That's all I can say! One crazy hen." And she went back to her grazing.

There remained the world of men, and for a while Hen occupied herself by observing Farmer Brown and his family. It didn't take Hen long to realize that God had programmed men just as he had programmed hens, but instead of unanswerable philosophical questions He had crammed men's minds with a passion for things. During one weekend Hen checked off the following things being carried into Farmer Brown's house: a Carrier room air conditioner, two dresses from the Especially Yours Dressmaking Shop, a Boston rocker in very poor condition from the Den of Antiquity, some crocheting material from the Nook 'N Cranny Needlecraft Shop, a bow and some arrows from the Pro-Staff Archery Center, a fiberglass boat from Midwest Marine, three cases of Dr. Pepper from the Soda Boy Pop Shop, a Figurette bra and girdle from Merle Norman Cosmetics & Boutiques, a set of cooking utensils from Saladmaster, a lawn mower from Simplicity Garden-Lawn Equipment, a football from Spartan Sporting Goods, a plumber's helper from K-Mart, a piano given to the Browns by a relative who no longer played it, pictures of the kids from Ziph Photography, a set of peach colored slip covers from Penney's, a red plastic fire truck with a bell attached from Woolco's, Easy Street shoes (two pair) from LaMode, a blonde wig from Venus Wig Salon, a tapestry showing three deer drinking from a stream from American Wallpaper & Paint Company and a Sony U-matic Color Videocassette from Sony Video.

Listening at the kitchen window, Hen heard Mrs. Brown say, "Elmer, I need more things. Not only that, but Belinda needs more things. Jimmy told me the other day that he needs more things. Mary's new baby needs some things. My mother phoned yesterday to tell me she needs some things. My sister Susan wrote from Alabama to tell me she needed some things. George and Ethel are coming for dinner Sunday and I'll have to get some things. I need to get some things for Eva and some things for Gwen. Mildred's having her shower next week and I'll have to get her something. I have to get some things for the bathroom. I looked in the pantry this morning and we're out of everything. I don't have a thing to wear and unless I get to the store we won't have a thing to eat. What do you think of that?"

Farmer Brown thought about it for a minute, buttered a roll, put it into his mouth, ate it and replied, "*I need some things!*"

Hen also observed that when the Browns were not busy buying things, they were watching other human beings on the TV who were competing on game shows for things. An entire pasture had been covered to a height of seven feet with discarded things, but the Browns wanted more. A creek which had once run free and clear in the sunlight was clogged with old auto bodies, washing machines, refrigerators, home freezers, blenders, crock pots, pressure cookers, fry pans, vacuum cleaners, coffee makers, garbage disposals, sofas, easy chairs, beds, carpets, but no one seemed satisfied. What's more, Hen perceived, no one would ever be satisfied because each of these objects had been designed to provide no ultimate satisfaction. Finally, Hen flopped down exhausted in the dust by the side of the road between a smashed up 1957 Dodge and a broken Amana Microwave oven and uttered what would turn out to be her final prayer.

"Dear God, I once begged you not to cast me into the body of a hen, but I was wrong. Hens are fools and they lead stupid, useless lives, but one creature is worse and that is Man. I thank you now most profoundly, from the bottom of my chicken's heart, for not forcing my spirit into the body of a human being, for of all things on this earth human beings are the most confused, the most subject to illusions unworthy of a creature created by God. If you will take me now, I'll ascend happily into heaven and go gladly for the hundred and second time into the body of a hen again. And I know that because you do in fact value justice you will do this for me. But please, God, whatever you decide to do with me, don't thrust me into the body of a human being, for that would be a fate worse than the one I deserve. Yours truly, your obedient servant, Hen."

Hen fell asleep immediately after this to dream that her wings had grown to enormous proportions, extending outward from her body by ten or twelve feet. And her feathers were no longer hen's feathers but seemed now to be made from some silky substance akin to the down which issues from the milkweed pod. They were tipped with pink and blue and the colors intensified minute by minute because, as Hen could see, the sun was rising magnificently on the horizon, washing everything in a vibrant light. A breeze sprang up, carrying with it the smell of fresh spring-water and of the catkins from birch trees, and then Hen was rising, borne up by the breeze. She rose above the level of the roadside hedges, above the level of the poplar trees in Farmer Brown's windbreak, above the windmill slowly revolving beside the barn. She saw her hen's body below her on the ground and knew that she had left it for good. This was no dream and the spirit was going home, to be judged and to be given its punishment or reward. Second by second as the spirit mounted up, God's face came closer. As it flew over the lip of the first cloud it noticed, with a feeling of foreboding, that God was not smiling.

James Hennigan woke with a terrific headache which, he discovered, no amount of aspirin could do anything to mitigate. This had happened before and it sometimes marked the onset of one of his creative periods. For James was a poet, a famous one, and his creative periods always paid off for him, to the extent of five books of poetry (*Tiny Beasts*, National Book Award, 1967), three novels (*Grim City*, Hilda M. Lillienthal Award, 1969), a prestigious position at a major Midwestern university, some power, a little money, property, a wife and two children, two automobiles, a boat and a cabin in the woods. "A migraine, a migraine," he told his wife. "You know what that means! One of my creative periods is coming on. Call the university and tell them I don't intend to come in today. And then ... And then you know what to do!" His wife, who had been through it before, picked up the children and left the house. As soon as he heard the station wagon turn out of the driveway and onto the street, James Hennigan began to throw things. His rage increased and he overturned chairs, tore the mattress off the bed in the master bedroom, smashed a glass bell with a Norman Rockwell painting on it his mother had sent him for Christmas, lifted the books from the bookcase and heaved them at the wall, kicked in the television set, ripped some Kandinsky prints down and tossed them into the fireplace and shattered a piece of porcelain by throwing it into the kitchen sink. "Oh, this is going to be a good one!" he cried, kicking a hole in the sofa. "This is going to be fine, just fine!" Weeping came in right on schedule. Then he felt himself being split in two and a Self he had never known before began to speak out of his shattered sense of being. And this Self had been there since the moment of birth, he realized, always latent in the flesh, through all the phases of his existence from Little Jimmie to Jim to James to James Hennigan, Ph.D. (University of Minnesota, Harvard, Kenyon.) Now he began to squeak, flapping his arms and jumping up and down, tears streaming down his face. "Oh God," he cried. "What would you have me do?"

When the fit subsided, he crawled exhausted, trembling, bathed in sweat to his typewriter, which was sitting undisturbed amid the debris, illuminated by a curious white light. There he typed out what he knew to be the most profound truth to which he had ever borne witness: "GOD—IS—A—HARDBOILED—EGG!"

MOUSE

MICE KNOW ONLY ONE COLOR and that color is gray. The word for "color" in mouse language—"tikki"—is also the word for gray. It's been said that there was one mouse a long time ago who saw another color (I think it was brown), but I don't believe it. The word for "cat" and the word for "death" is "i-tikki," which can be translated as "the sudden absence of gray" or "annihilation." Many mice welcome it when it comes.

In a previous incarnation, I was Richard W. Hovey of St. Joseph, Missouri. I was employed by the Wire

Rope Corporation as a foreman. I had three children, two girls and a boy. My wife's name was Anita and she outlived me by seven years. It's not very interesting being a mouse, but it wasn't very interesting being Richard W. Hovey of St. Joseph, Missouri either.

Everyone eats mice—hawks, owls, coyotes, foxes, you name it. Mice are the universal food. We were made to be eaten. When, because of some ecological imbalance, there are no creatures around to eat us, we get very restless and depressed, and after a while we commit suicide. Then our spirits (such as they are) go up to heaven and are reincarnated again, almost always as mice. As food, we are simply too good to be true. Some say we taste like roast beef; others say it's more like lamb. I have even heard us compared to New England boiled dinner. There's no accounting for taste.

While we mice are apparently gourmet food for all other creatures, we ourselves have undeveloped palates and will eat almost anything, with the possible exception of brussels sprouts. Indeed, we must eat at least three times our weight in grain every day of our lives or die. So there are no real restaurants in Mouse Land, only pit stop drive-ins, similar to your own McDonald's. We mice spend so much time eating, we seldom do anything else. A friend of mine (now deceased) once organized a whist party, but no one came. They were too busy eating.

Sex for mice is quick, remarkably efficient and not particularly interesting. We have no mating calls, no courtship rituals, no dances and of course no colorful plumage (since we have no sense of color). We simply do it as quickly as possible, get it over with and go on eating. They say that over 80 billion mice are born on the planet earth every year. It's a wise mouse that knows its own father.

We mice are eternal lookers-on. We have witnessed most of the major events in human history. We were there, for instance, when Ben Franklin discovered radium, when the Buddha turned water into wine and when Attila the Hun won the Battle of Borodino. Some say we mice are in such an infernal hurry, we can never pause long enough to get our facts straight. But I have just proved to you that that particular aspersion is incorrect. People are always putting down mice and it's unfair. We're as good as anyone else. Just give us a chance.

Few mice live on into old age, but one who did, Rik-tuk-ti, a Tibetan mouse, attained wisdom. However, only one of his sayings has come down to us: "My fellow mice, it isn't worth it." Thus, Rik-tuk-ti. It is generally believed that Rik-tuk-ti died when accidentally stepped upon by a yak. But I believe that he was decapitated in a whirling prayer wheel. All we know for certain is that Rik-tuk-ti saw into the heart of things and that it made him unhappy. Most mice are unhappy, but Rik-tuk-ti was unhappier than most. If there were state institutions for depressed mice, most of us would commit ourselves.

Mice never laugh. In that respect, mice are like moles, who never laugh either. Rats have been known to laugh, but never mice. Other creatures make jokes in the presence of mice, but mice always miss the point. Mice don't get invited out to parties very much. In the last hundred years, only one invitation has ever been extended to a mouse, and that was from a bantam rooster who didn't know any better. If mice could sing, they'd sing the blues. But mice can't sing. We mice sulk a lot. It's understandable, given our situation. But you can't really expect the other animals to sympathize with us. They have problems of their own.

I hope that in my next incarnation, my spirit manifests itself in a bluebird. I think that if they were honest with themselves, most mice would admit that they would rather be bluebirds. Bluebirds can fly. Bluebirds can sing. And bluebirds can see another color beyond gray, namely blue—the color (they tell me) of the precious stone used in the construction of the ramparts of Heaven. But I have no real hope of being reincarnated as a bluebird. I glanced at my records the last time I made the Great Journey around the Wheel and I saw that I had 15,972,412 more incarnations to go, and that in every single incarnation I was a mouse.

As you can see, I'm caught like a mouse in a trap, and the trap has cosmic dimensions. And the worst thing is, I don't even have time to stop, sit down and figure out who's to blame. If you find out, let me know. Now forgive me, but I've got to run. Goodbye.

PEACOCK

TAKE IT FROM ME, *ma petite poule*, God has a truly wicked sense of humor. To punish me for sins He claims I committed in a previous lifetime, He has metamorphosed me into this gross, gravel-voiced, overweight bird! He has done this to me, to *me*!—who loved the ballet, the German *lied*, the poetry of Swinburne and epicene young jockeys! And He has placed me here in Golden Gate Park, of all places. Day and night I feel His foot on the shafts of my fantail, hear His voice in the brittle rustling of my train, sense His eyes focused eternally on my opalescent bun-buns. Off my ass, God! I've had it with you. You made me what I am today (as you made me what I was yesterday) and I refuse to feel guilty about it. Nor will I mount those simpering peahens again, subservient to your insane demands. Fertilize those damned eggs without me. I'm through!

But I must admit, strictly *entre nous*, that being re-incarnated as a peacock has its moments. Take "con-sciousness," for example. To experience the world through the consciousness of a peacock is to live with shattered rainbows, smashed prisms and tumbling color-wheels. Sometimes my spirit seems pierced with shards of green jade. Exquisite sensations, sunset ecstacies! Oscar Wilde would have adored it. But oh, how I long for the old days and for that human life I threw away, never knowing the real value of the precious gift I'd been given. But enough of that.

I was born Henry L. Montmorency in Charleston, South Carolina, on July 17, 1873. The "L" stood for "Legare." Yes, I was a "Legare," which meant some-thing in Charleston in those days. No one believed that a creature so sickly could survive in that climate. You've heard of blue babies? Well, *I* emerged from the womb a positive mauve! Mauve! That particular shade of ani-line dye was just about to become the rage, so I was high fashion from the very beginning, don't you see? Someone told my mother that the cure for infant colic was champagne, so I was given liberal doses of the stuff from the beginning, and I survived. Yes, I survived, to wear red velvet suits with collars of Belgian lace on trips to Europe with Mama! Survived, to disrupt some of the best preparatory schools in France and Switzerland! Survived, to marry a woman about whom I remember nothing except that she had a passion for camellias and placed a bag of sachet under my pillow on our wedding night. My conversion to Catholicism grew out of my passion for incense, robes, ostentatious ceremony and choir boys. When Papa threatened to disinherit me, I dropped Catholicism immediately in favor of laudanum, absinthe, decadent poetry, Paris and sex. I died of an overdose of opium in Lausanne in December, 1907. I know the family said I drowned in a boating accident on Lake Geneva, but that was simply a cover-up. My body, packed in ice, was shipped home on the Mauretania and interred in Magnolia Cemetery. My spirit was buried in the bird you see before you now.

As I look out at you with my hooded eyes, I see a young barbarian—tanned, bearded, barefoot, wearing dirty walking shorts and carrying a can of beer. Only one thought crosses your mind—if you can call it a mind!—"What a weird looking bird!" You don't even know that I'm called a "peacock." Nor do you care. Soon you'll turn away, eager to get to Marx Meadow and the Fair there. Civilization has crumbled away! When I cruised the Lido seventy years ago I wore a white suit tailored in London, shoes hand-crafted in Holland, a wide-brimmed hat with a pongee of Indian silk and puce gloves fitted to my hands in Berlin. Unless my eyes deceive me, you aren't even wearing underpants! But you've lost so much, dear boy, with your so-called "liberation." What's happened to those subtle distinctions of class, of breeding? And there are so many things you'll never know—the infinite varieties of madness, of mental aberration, of lunacy growing out of all that repression. Art, religion, philosophy, theology—all grew out of sublimation! What have you replaced them with? Backpacking and baseball! It makes me want to scream! And yet, I remember a time in Oujda in Morocco, when a woman brought her brother to me, a boy no older than twelve, smelling of the animals he tended, without a thought in his mind beyond the physical pleasure he could give me. What did I care about civilization then? And as for my clothes, my greatest moments came when I could get out of them and romp around in the buff!

Now you turn away, bored with me, and move off toward the meadow, leaving me here by myself, making awkward, piercing noises so gross and obscene they shiver the leaves on the eucalyptus trees around me.

WORM

"Tell me, Brother, what do you see?" said Mrs. Noah to the lowly worm.
—Robert Duncan, "The Ballad of Mrs. Noah"

I SEE YOUR TOES, MRS. NOAH, which look remarkably like worms to me. I see the brass ring on your big toe, which looks like a worm biting its own tail. I see dirt between your toes, which makes me long for home. In short, I see toes, toes, toes—for I am a worm, and worms were designed to stare at toes. And what do I see when I look beyond you? I see the sea which surrounds

66

this boat. I see the sky, which is intensely blue. High above I see the beady, inquisitive eye of a bird, and ordinarily I would be apprehensive, but I know that the Creator has put Death in irons for the duration of this cruise. In the depths of the sky I see my Maker polishing his lamps. He has always been kind to me. The least things satisfy me—air, earth, water—and he gives me these things in abundance. I am elemental. I was here first. First the earth, then the worm to nuzzle that earth with love. All other creatures came later, even the serpent, who is my cousin and is modeled on me. Some say the world rests on a giant turtle, but believe me when I tell you it rests on me. I tunnel in the fecund earth: *worm, womb, woman*. Sperm is my brother. All creation begins and ends with me, the lowly worm.

Call me *digger*. I will dig through your guts. Call me *transformer*. There you go, thanks to me, metamorphosed into an acacia tree, or flowing into a date palm, or filling the corm of a gladiolus. Magician of the clay, I go about my business among the roots and bulbs. Now, looking down at me from way up there, tell me, what do you see, Mother Noah?

Worm, I see the goat's prick, the bull's pizzle, the sex of husband and sons. As I bend to lift you into the air, male comes to female, phallus to omphalos, beginning to end. In a sudden blaze of noon, illuminated, I kneel to worship—Worm.

Everything That Has Been Shall Be Again
is the first published collection of the reincarnation fables
of John Gilgun. This edition is reproduced from proofs
of a limited edition hand printed at The Bieler Press.